"HELLO READING books are a perfect introduction to ing. Brief sentences full of word repetition and full-color pictures stress visual clues to help a child take the first important steps toward reading. Mastering these story books will build children's reading confidence and give them the enthusiasm to stand on their own in the world of words."

—Bee Cullinan
Past President of the International Reading
Association, Professor in New York University's
Early Chil

813
Zi

Ziefert, Harriet
AUTHOR

Let's Trade
TITLE

Br i ood a

813
Zi

"Readers aren't bo
by parents who w

"When I was a
importance of go
reading is more
dren who have
reading. They a
comprehension.
stories grows ou

M.

For Lynn Seiffer

PUFFIN BOOKS
Published by the Penguin Group
Viking Penguin Inc., 40 West 23rd Street, New York, New York 10010, U.S.A.
Penguin Books Ltd, 27 Wrights Lane, London W8 5TZ, England
Penguin Books Australia Ltd, Ringwood, Victoria, Australia
Penguin Books Canada Ltd, 2801 John Street, Markham, Ontario, Canada L3R 1B4
Penguin Books (N.Z.) Ltd, 182-190 Wairau Road, Auckland 10, New Zealand

Penguin Books Ltd, Registered Offices: Harmondsworth, Middlesex, England

First published in Puffin Books, 1989 • Published simultaneously in Canada

1 3 5 7 9 10 8 6 4 2

Text copyright © Harriet Ziefert, 1989
Illustrations copyright © Mary Morgan, 1989
All rights reserved
Library of Congress catalog card number: 88-62150
ISBN 0-14-050982-8

Printed in Singapore for Harriet Ziefert, Inc.

Let's Trade

Harriet Ziefert
Pictures by Mary Morgan

PUFFIN BOOKS

"Have a nice picnic!"
said Mom.

Meg, Sam, and Jo
took their lunch bags.

Then they went to the park.
Their cat went, too.

"I have a pickle and
grapes," said Meg.
"Sam, what do you have?"

"I have a banana,"
said Sam.
"And I'm sick of bananas!"

"I like bananas," said Meg.
"Let's trade."

Sam gave Meg the banana.
Meg gave Sam the pickle.

"What do you have?"
Meg asked Jo.

"I have peanut butter," said Jo.
"I'm sick of peanut butter!"

"I like peanut butter," said Meg.
"Let's trade."

Jo gave Meg the sandwich.
Meg gave Jo grapes.

"What do you have?"
Jo asked Meg.

"I have a banana and
I have peanut butter,"
said Meg.

"But you have *two* things!"
said Sam and Jo together.
"It's not fair!"

"I'll be fair!" said Meg.
"I'll share!"

Meg shared the banana.
Meg shared the sandwich.

"Now you have more than me!"
Meg said to Sam and Jo.
"You each have *three* things!"

Sam ate the pickle
and the peanut butter—
but *not* the banana!

"Remember," he said,
"I'm sick of bananas!"

Jo ate the grapes
and the banana—
but *not* the peanut butter.

"Remember," she said,
"I'm sick of peanut butter!"

Meg put her banana on top
of the peanut butter.
She ate it all up.
"Yummy!" she said.

"Yuck!" said Sam.
"Yuck!" said Jo.

"You wanted *my* food," said Meg.
"Now eat it all up!"

"I won't!" said Sam.
"I won't eat banana!"

"I won't," said Jo.
"I won't eat peanut butter."

"Just listen to me," said Meg.

"Sam, trade with Jo.
Jo, trade with Sam."

"You're bossy!" said Sam to Meg.
But he ate the peanut butter.